A patch of spring sunshine is a pleasant place to read.

"Why does Dave keep looking at me like that?" asked Kate's dad.

"Because you're in his chair, Daddy, just where it's warm," said Kate.

For Dee

"All dogs's good dogs."
—*Jack Biggs, dog owner*

Text and illustrations © 2007 by Blackbird Design Pty Ltd.

First U.S. paperback edition 2010

The Library of Congress has cataloged the hardcover edition as follows:

Graham, Bob, date.
  "The trouble with dogs," said Dad / Bob Graham. — 1st U.S. ed.
    p.   cm.
  Sequel to: "Let's get a pup!" said Kate.
  Summary: When a dog trainer is called in to teach Dave the dog how to behave, Dave isn't the only one who learns something new.
  ISBN 978-0-7636-3316-5 (hardcover)
  [1. Dogs—Fiction. 2. Dogs—Training—Fiction.] I. Title.
  PZ7.G751667Tro 2007
  [E]—dc22   2007000896

ISBN 978-0-7636-4973-9 (paperback)

10 11 12 13 14 15
TWPS 10 9 8 7 6 5 4 3 2 1

Printed in Singapore

This book was typeset in Bulmer.
The illustrations were done in ink and watercolor.

Candlewick Press
99 Dover Street
Somerville, Massachusetts 02144

visit us at www.candlewick.com

CANDLEWICK PRESS

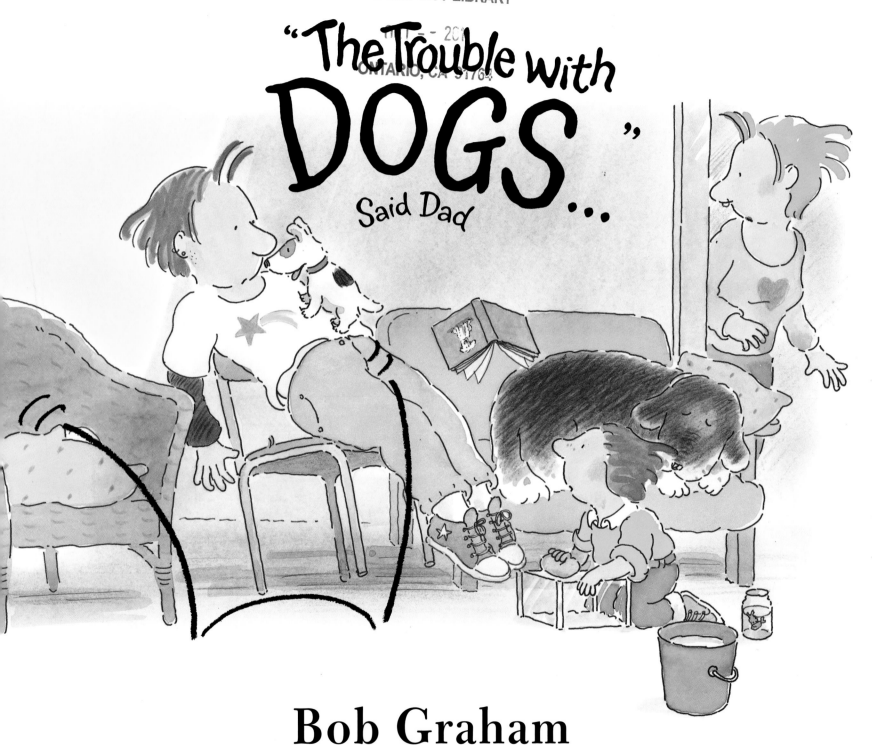

"The Trouble with DOGS..." Said Dad

Bob Graham

"The trouble with dogs," said Dad,
"is that they take over your life.
    Run the show."

"What show?" Kate asked,
    then right away forgot her question.
"Look," she said. "When I rub Rosy like
    this . . . her foot scratches like this."

"Interesting," said Dad.
"Hmm," said Mom.
    And they all gazed in love and admiration
    at Rosy, brought home from the
    Rescue Center eight months ago.

While Rosy was large and soft,

as comfortable to lie on as an old sofa and endlessly patient . . .

Dave was small and wild. He slipped and he slid;

he leaped and he skittered. He was take-me-as-you-find-me, don't-care Dave.

"He's so . . . exuberant!" said Dad.

"What's that?" asked Kate.

"Excited," said Dad.

"Joyful," added Mom.

And they all gazed at Dave,

brought home along with Rosy.

"Full of the joys of spring!" said Mom.

Spring turned to summer
and Dave was still . . . well . . . Dave!

In the park, he cut a picnic party
clean in two and ran right down
the middle of the flower beds,
just to show it could be done.
"Dave needs a firmer hand," said Mom.
"Someone to tell him no."

They all looked at Dad.
"No, Dave," he said.
"No, Dave," Mom called a little louder.
"No, Dave!" said Kate
as he jumped up to lick her on the nose.

Summer drew to a close,
but there was still no
change in Dave.

He often tied Kate in knots,
left small puddles on
the kitchen floor,

and tore holes in
the tights of her school friends.

Then one day, he jumped uninvited onto a guest's lap
and ate a cupcake right off her plate.

"We need help!" said Dad.

Mom went to the phone book.

"Look," she said.

PUP BREAKERS

We Tame Troublesome Beasts!

For barkers, biters, breakers and bumpers, post sniffers, leaping leash-tanglers, and small dogs who smell nameless spots on the grass and won't move . . .

We can take the pounce from your pup, the bounce from your bunny, or the squawk from your caged bird.

Especially for owners so meek and mild that they can't say "Boo!" to a grasshopper.

Telephone: 555-216-1625

"That's us!" said Dad.

"Let's call them," said Mom.

The next day, there stood
the Brigadier at 9 a.m. sharp.
"What seems to be the
problem?" he asked.
They all looked at Dave,
who had a fresh garden flower
hanging from his mouth.

"That dog needs lessons,"
said the Brigadier. "Right now!
Lesson one . . . is just one word."
A bird twittered nervously.
"One simple little word:

No!"

It knocked the breath
out of all of them.
Dave dropped the flower,
wet and glistening,
to the path.

"Head up, chin in, chest out,

   back straight," barked the Brigadier.

"Lesson two . . .

Here!"

"Who . . . me?" asked Mom.

"No, madam, the pup,"

   replied the Brigadier.

"Oh, you mean Dave!" said Mom.

"David, here!"

"Lesson three," the Brigadier went on.
"The slip chain. Threaded just so and
placed carefully around the neck, it will
enable you (with a short, sharp jerk) to
control your animal.

Ready, David?"

Dave did heel work,

leash work,

and sit work.

He trotted,

he stayed,

and then he came.

But no one had the heart for
a "short, sharp jerk" on that chain.

At last the Brigadier said,
"We're finished for today.
I'll be back next week
to polish off the rough edges."
He clicked the gate shut
like a trap as Rosy attended
to some tiny creature deep in
a crease on the inside of her leg.

"What rough edges?" asked Kate.
"Dave has nothing but soft
and squashy bits."
Dad didn't say a word.
Nor did Mom.

In the days that followed,
a change came
over Dave.

"The trouble is,"
said Dad, "he's
lost his sparkle."

"The trouble is," said Mom,
"he's lost his crackle and fizz."

"The trouble," said Kate,
"is the Brigadier's lessons."

The next week came around and so did the Brigadier.

"Let's get started!" he shouted.

Dave shivered, but he didn't run away.

Instead he tiptoed slowly forward. . . .

"He's saying he's glad to see you," said Mom.

"To see *me*?" said the Brigadier.

And then something extraordinary happened.

The man from Pup Breakers smiled.

At least Kate *thought* he smiled.

It was difficult to see under his mustache.

"I think we should have some tea," said Mom.

"And I think we should tell him," Kate said quietly.

"Tell me what?" asked the Brigadier.
Kate blinked, then said, "That Dave
doesn't need lessons anymore."
"And why is that, young Kate?"
"Because . . ." Kate whispered, "because
I think shouting hurts Dave's feelings and
we should always be polite to our dogs."

There was silence.

Then all at once
Dave slipped past Mom.
He slid and he skittered
and he leaped . . .

right up onto the Brigadier's
lap and ate the cupcake
off his plate.

Then another extraordinary
thing happened.
"Perhaps you're right, Kate,"
the Brigadier said. "Perhaps
we shouldn't shout at our dogs."

He patted Dave's head.

"You're a cute little fella,"

he whispered.

"Share the crumbs with Rosy."

And then he left.

"The *real* trouble with dogs," said Dad
the next day, "is that their ears are
so silky. If you lay Dave's ears across
your knees — and stroke them like this —
have you ever done that?"
Kate nodded. "Lots," she said.
Dave wagged his tail.
"All the time," added Mom.
Rosy's stomach rumbled.
She fell asleep and snored.

By the following spring, Kate has grown a little more.

"Just move the chairs, Daddy," she says.

"Brilliant idea, Kate!" says Dad. Now the sun warms them both.